Daylight Starlight

WILDLIFE

WENDELL MINOR

Nancy Paulsen Books ☮ An Imprint of Penguin Group (USA)

The sun shines on Earth, bringing the light and warmth of day. Do you know these daylight visitors?

Then Earth spins away from
the sun, bringing the darkness
and cool of night. Do you know
these starlight visitors?

By day, sharp-eyed red-tailed hawk
soars high in the sky and scans
the earth for food.

In the stillness of night,
wide-eyed barn owl silently
swoops through the sky.

At dawn, fluffy cottontail rabbit
and her kits hop into the field
and hold still till all is safe.

At night, pink-nosed opossum
plods through the field and forages
for food with her family on her back.

Bright tiger swallowtail
butterfly floats and flutters
in the summer sunshine.

Named for the moon,
luminous luna moth
only comes out at night.

Graceful white-tailed deer finds her fawn
hiding in the flower-filled field.

On a frigid night, crafty red fox carefully
listens, then crouches and quickly pounces.

Chubby mother woodchuck
and her cubs waddle out
to munch in the meadow.

Fearless mother skunk leads
her litter through the field
to find a midnight snack.

Speedy gray squirrel scurries
all day in search of acorns
to store for winter.

Flying squirrel glides
gracefully from tree to tree
through the starlit night.

Brightly colored box turtle shuffles through the tall grass, searching for slugs, snails, and strawberries.

Warty toad will stick out his sticky tongue
to slurp down a nighttime meal of moths.

Small striped chipmunk perches
on a pumpkin to fill his cheeks
with goodies from the garden.

Sprightly deer mouse scampers
down a log and finds a firefly.

As the sun rises, stealthy bobcat and her kitten scope out the summer landscape.

On a cold winter's night, clever coyote
howls beneath the stars to call to his pack.

Colorful red cardinal
welcomes the sunrise
with a sweet song.

As night falls, the song of
brown-eyed barred owl fills
the forest—*hoo-hoo, hoo-hoo,
hoo-hoo, hoo-hoo-aw*.

As our world turns from night to day, critters
big and small come and go. While you're resting,
are raccoons racing by under the cover of night?

Who knows what the light of morning will bring? Look and listen. What wonderful wildlife is visiting you?

FUN FACTS

All the wildlife featured in *Daylight Starlight Wildlife* has visited my backyard at one time or another. No matter where you live, chances are you may have seen or heard many of them too. Some are diurnal (daytime), some are nocturnal (nighttime), and some are crepuscular (twilight—sunrise and/or sunset). Here are some interesting facts about the creatures in this book.

 Red-tailed hawks are the most common hawks in North America. They like to soar over open fields, and with their very keen eyesight, they can easily spot a mouse while in flight. *Diurnal*

 Barn owls are silent in flight due to their soft fringe-edged feathers. They have excellent hearing for hunting in the darkest of nights. *Nocturnal*

 Cottontail rabbits mostly hop along slowly, but if they are spotted by a predator, they can run up to 18 miles an hour. *Crepuscular*

 Opossums are the only marsupials (pouched mammals) native to the United States. Baby opossums stay in their mother's pouch for the first few months, then ride on her back until they are ready to hunt on their own. *Nocturnal*

 Tiger swallowtail butterflies have yellow and black stripes resembling a tiger's, and long tails on each hind wing that resemble a swallow's. *Diurnal*

 *Luna moths* are sometimes called moon moths. They have no mouth and cannot feed, so they live for only a few days, and are a rare sight. *Nocturnal*

 *White-tailed deer* mothers are protective of their young. While they forage for food, their fawns stay hidden nearby, camouflaged against the forest floor. *Crepuscular*

 Red foxes stalk their prey and often pounce to catch them. Their excellent hearing allows them to easily pinpoint the location of their prey. *Nocturnal, but active early morning and late evening*

 Woodchucks, also known as groundhogs, put on weight in spring and summer to store energy for winter hibernation. A woodchuck can eat a whole pound of vegetation in one sitting! *Diurnal*

 Skunks look very distinctive with their black-and-white furry coats. When threatened, skunks release a pungent-smelling spray to ward off any enemies. *Nocturnal*

Gray squirrels come in a variety of shades of gray, black, orange, and brown. They are very noisy for their size, often barking and chattering, and can eat two pounds of nuts a week. *Diurnal*

 Flying squirrels have a special membrane between their front and back legs that allows them to glide through the air like a kite. They have very large black eyes that help them see at night. *Nocturnal*

 Box turtles have a beautiful dome-shaped shell with yellow, orange, black, and/or olive markings. These turtles can live up to 80 years. *Diurnal*

 *American toads* live on the land as adults, but start their life as tadpoles in water. Toads eat spiders, slugs, earthworms, and lots of insects. *Nocturnal*

 *Chipmunks* have cheek pouches that can enlarge to three times bigger than their heads. They are used to transport food. *Diurnal*

 Deer mice are plentiful, and female deer mice can have many litters in one year. They are adept climbers and like to play at night in woodland areas. *Nocturnal*

 Bobcats are named for their short bobbed tail. These wildcats are excellent hunters who are very territorial. A typical bobcat litter will have one to six kittens. *Nocturnal and diurnal*

 Coyotes have very keen vision and a sharp sense of smell, making them expert hunters. They howl to communicate and to keep track of their family. *Nocturnal, sometimes crepuscular*

 Cardinals have 16 different calls, but their most familiar call is their classic "cheer, cheer, cheer." The male cardinal is known for its brilliant red color, while the brown females have a sharp crest and red accents. *Diurnal*

 Barred owls are named for the distinctive stripes on their breast. Their night call sounds like the pattern of the words "who cooks for you?" *Nocturnal*

 Wild turkeys have 20 different calls, including their unique "gobble, gobble" sound. They can fly up to 55 miles per hour, but only for short distances. *Diurnal*

 Raccoons have a distinctive black "mask" across their eyes. They are very smart foragers and have learned how to take the lids off trash cans and unlatch doors. *Nocturnal*

"If you truly love nature, you will find beauty everywhere."—Vincent van Gogh

In memory of Matthew Cowles and his love for all things wild and free, and to his grandson, Max, who will carry on in his spirit—W.M.

Acknowledgments

Thanks to my photographer friends, Robert Shaw and Leo Kulinsky, for the use of their wildlife photos as reference sources for some of the art in this book.

Internet Sources

National Wildlife Federation • www.nwf.org/How-to-Help/Garden-for-Wildlife/Create-a-Habitat.aspx
and www.nwf.org/How-to-Help/Garden-for-Wildlife/Schoolyard-Habitats.aspx
Washington Department of Fish and Wildlife • wdfw.wa.gov/living/attracting/
Santa Barbara Museum of Natural History • www.sbnature.org/content/663/file/backyardcrittersMar2011.pdf

Nancy Paulsen Books
Published by the Penguin Group
Penguin Group (USA) LLC
375 Hudson Street, New York, NY 10014

USA | Canada | UK | Ireland | Australia | New Zealand | India | South Africa | China
penguin.com
A Penguin Random House Company

Library of Congress Cataloging-in-Publication Data
Minor, Wendell, author. Daylight starlight wildlife / Wendell Minor.   pages cm
Summary: "An introduction to diurnal (daytime) and nocturnal (nighttime) animals"—Provided by publisher.
Audience: Ages 3–5. 1. Animal behavior—Miscellanea—Juvenile literature. 2. Nocturnal animals—Juvenile literature. I. Title.
QL751.5.M56 2015   591.5´1—dc23   2014036195
Manufactured in China by South China Printing Co. Ltd.
ISBN 978-0-399-24662-3
1 3 5 7 9 10 8 6 4 2

Design by Annie Ericsson. Text set in LTC Cloister.
The art was done in gouache and watercolor on Strathmore paper.

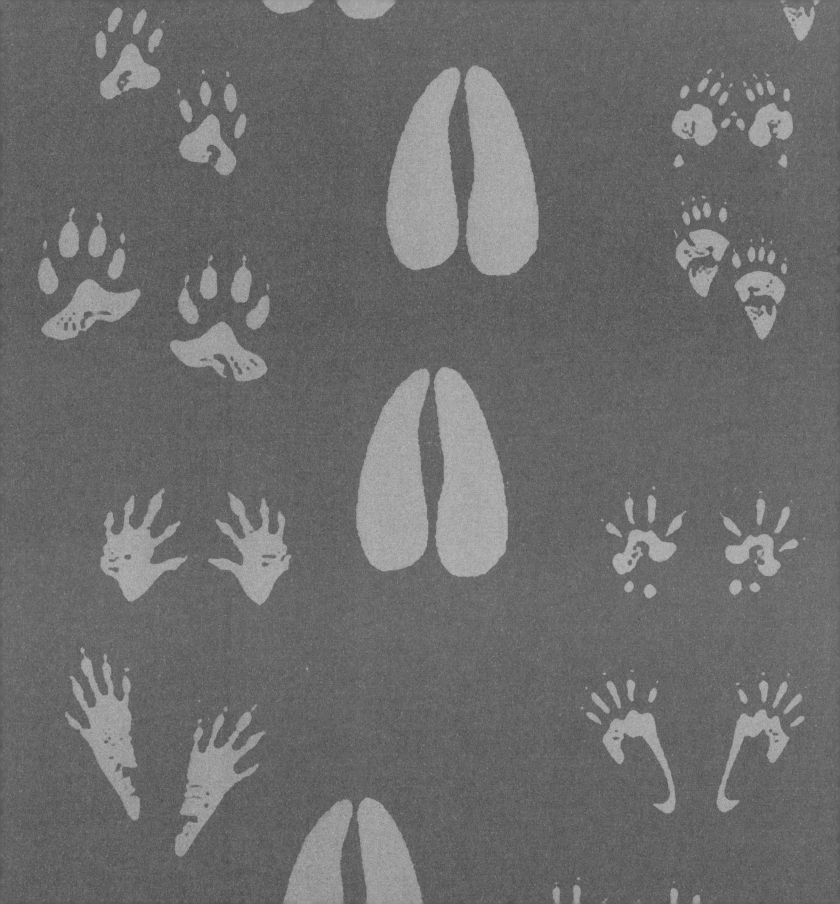